ROVER SAVES CHRISTMAS

RODDY DOYLE

Have you read
Roddy Doyle's
first fantastic
children's book?

THE GIGGLER TREATMENT

ROVER SAVES CHRISTMAS

RODDY DOYLE

Illustrated by Brian Ajhar

SCHOLASTIC
PRESS

Scholastic Children's Books,
Commonwealth House, 1-19 New Oxford Street,
London WC1A 1NU, UK
a division of Scholastic Ltd
London ~ New York ~ Toronto ~ Sydney ~ Auckland
Mexico City ~ New Delhi ~ Hong Kong

First published by Scholastic Ltd, 2001

Copyright © Roddy Doyle, 2001
Cover illustration copyright © Charlie Fuge, 2001
Inside illustrations copyright © Brian Ajhar, 2001

ISBN 0 439 99398 9

Printed by Bath Press

1 3 5 7 9 10 8 6 4 2

The right of Roddy Doyle to be identified as the author
of this work has been asserted by him in accordance
with the Copyright, Designs and Patents Act, 1988.

To Santa

Thanks to Abel Ugba for his advice,
and to Thomas Gromoff, for
the Finnish word for "poo".
R.D.

To Rebecca Lynn
B.A.

CHAPTER ONE

It was Christmas Eve in Dublin and the sun was splitting the rocks. The lizards were wearing flip-flops and the cacti that line the streets of the city were gasping.

"Water!" gasped a cactus.

"Diet water!" gasped his girlfriend beside him.

The River Liffey had dried up and the tyres on all the city's buses had melted. Robbie and Jimmy Mack were frying an egg on a shovel and—

Hang on.

Yes?

Dublin isn't like that at Christmas. Start again.

OK.

It was Christmas Eve in Dublin and it had been snowing for weeks. Snow-flakes the size of mice fell from the grey sky and the cacti that line the streets of the city were very cold and confused. Jimmy and Robbie Mack were trying to scrape a frozen egg off a shovel and—

Stop.

Yes?

Dublin isn't like that either. Stop being silly or I won't buy the book.

Sorry.

It was Christmas Eve in Dublin and it was raining. It had been raining for weeks and the cacti that line the streets of the city were sick of it.

"I'm full," said a cactus.

"I'm fat," said his girlfriend beside him.

Robbie and Jimmy Mack threw eggs at each other because there was no snow to make snowballs. One egg skidded on the wet grass and rolled under a wet, dripping bush. It stopped beside a lizard.

The lizard looked at the egg. He didn't want to eat it.

"Why not?" said the egg.

He was too cold to eat it. He was stiff and damp and miserable. He turned bright red, because he hoped that that would make him warm. But it didn't.

"What a lovely colour," said a voice beside him.

It was a lovely voice. It was the loveliest voice the lizard had ever heard. He looked, and saw the loveliest lizard he had ever seen. And he stayed red, because he was blushing.

"You look warm," said the loveliest lizard.

"Oh," said the lizard. "Actually, I'm very cold."

And, gradually, he stopped being red and became a much colder colour, grey.

"Are *you* not cold?" he said.

"No," said the loveliest lizard. "I have the right name."

"What do you mean?"

"Well," said the loveliest lizard. "I change my name whenever the weather changes. When it's very hot I choose a name from a hot country, and I feel fine. And when it's very cold or wet, like now, I choose a name from a colder country. What's *your* name?" she asked.

"Omar."

"Nice name," she said. "But not right for this weather. Try calling yourself 'Hans'. That's a nice cold name."

"OK," said Omar.

He coughed, and spoke. "My name is 'Hans'."

"How does that feel?" said the loveliest lizard.

Hans lowered his tummy down to the cold, wet grass.

"Nice," he said. "Very nice."

He rubbed his tummy on the grass. He began to glow; he was becoming silver. "Very, very nice. What's *your* name?" he asked.

"Heidi," said the loveliest lizard.

"Hi-dee-hi, Heidi," said Hans.

"Hi-dee-ho, Hans," said Heidi.

Hans flicked his long tongue and

caught a fly that was resting on a wall far away, in Morocco.

"Wow," said Heidi.

"Care to share some spicy wings?" said Hans.

Hans chewed and smiled at Heidi. Heidi chewed and smiled at Hans. They were full of fly and falling in love. But this story isn't about Hans and Heidi, although they're in it. And it definitely isn't about the fly. (He was tumbling down into Heidi's tummy, humming a sad song called "Torn Between Two Lizards".) The story is about Robbie and Jimmy and a dog and some other people and what they did on Christmas Eve.

It starts on the next page, Chapter Two. And that means that you just wasted your time reading Chapter One. Sorry.

CHAPTER TWO

Jimmy and Robbie Mack were very excited and very bored. It was Christmas Eve and they wanted the day to end, so they could go to bed and wake up the next morning.

Christmas Day.

The best day in the whole year.

They'd been thinking about nothing else for months.

"What do you want for breakfast?" their mother had asked Jimmy last October.

"Christmas," said Jimmy.

"What is the capital of France?" their teacher, Mister Eejit, had asked on the last day before the holidays.

"Presents," said Robbie.

Robbie and Jimmy had been extra-specially good for the last few weeks. For example, they had helped their Granda to find his false teeth. They were super-glued to the roof of his car. (Jimmy and Robbie had glued the teeth to the roof but it is much more important to know that they had helped poor old Granda to find them. And, by the way, they got the teeth off the roof with a can opener.) They'd spent all their pocket-money on presents for the people they loved – *Banjo-Kazooie* for their mother, a new uniform for Granny's Action Man, a special pair of scissors for their father for cutting the horrible big hairs that grew out of his ears and nose, a T-shirt with BARNEY SMOKES BIG FAT CIGARS on it for their baby sister and a brand new can opener for Granda. (The old one was stuck in the roof of his car.)

They had tied their stockings to the ends of their beds. They had made twenty-seven cheese sandwiches and left them in a huge pile on the mantelpiece for Santa. They had cut the crusts off the sandwiches because Santa never ate the crusts. And they

had left one of their mother's cans of Guinness on the mantelpiece beside the sandwiches, and a carrot for Rudolph.

But there were still hours and hours to go before bedtime.

"How long now?" said Jimmy.

"Thirteen hours and thirty-seven minutes," said Robbie.

"I think I'll make another sandwich for Santa."

"I think I'll peel Rudolph's carrot."

The brothers were walking to the back door. They were soaking wet and hungry and excited and bored and their little sister jumped out of an upstairs window of the house next-door.

CHAPTER THREE

Kayla Mack floated down under a parachute she'd made from half her best friend's mother's best dress. And Victoria, her best friend, followed her, hanging on to the other half of her mother's best dress.

It used to be a beautiful dress, and now it was two beautiful parachutes.

WARNING!

Don't try this at home, kids. Jumping out of upstairs windows is not a good idea. You could break your arm or your leg or your head or, if the window is shut, you could even break the glass. Also, in real life, dresses don't make good, safe parachutes, and half-dresses are even worse. So, don't jump, kids. Use the stairs. And, while we're at it, if you ever cut your mother's best dress in two, don't make parachutes out of it.

Just throw it in a corner and blame the cat. Leave the scissors beside the cat's mat and blow-dry his or her hair to make it look like he or she has been jumping out of aeroplanes all day. However, before you blame the cat, first make sure that you actually have one.

Now, back to the story.

It used to be a beautiful dress, and now it was two beautiful parachutes.

"Oh, man!" said Jimmy.

"Good on yourself, Kayla!" said Robbie.

They watched Kayla flying over their heads, carried on the wind. Her feet just missed the branches of an apple tree, and she landed in the centre of the garden, bang in the middle of the flower bed.

Robbie and Jimmy ran to congratulate her.

And then they saw the elf.

Because Kayla had landed on him.

"Get off me, please," said the elf.

"Who are you?" said Kayla.

"I'm too busy to answer that question," said the elf.

He looked very unhappy and wet. He was wearing a black leather jacket, with HELL'S ELVES printed on its back.

He got out from under Kayla, and Victoria landed on him.

"Get off me, please," said the elf. "I'm a busy man."

"Who are you?" said Kayla.

"Bum-bum," said Victoria.

"I told you," said the elf. "I'm too busy to answer."

"Who are you?"

"Bum-bum."

The elf took a notebook from the pocket of his jacket.

"Are you two being cheeky?" he said. "You'd better not be."

"Who are you?" said Kayla.

"That does it," said the elf. "You're going into me book. What's your name?"

"Who are you?"

"Bum-bum."

"What's your name?" said the elf.

"Who are you?"

"Bum-bum."

The elf took a pencil out from behind his very big ear. By the way, his other ear was very big too, and there was an earring hanging from it — a very small silver ear.

"Who are you?" said Kayla.

INTERRUPTION

You're probably wondering why Kayla kept saying, "Who are you?"

Well, the answer is easy.

She couldn't say anything else.

BACK TO
CHAPTER THREE

The elf flicked through the notebook.
"Who are you?" said Kayla.

RETURN OF THE
INTERRUPTION

Sorry for interrupting again but you need to know a little bit more about Kayla. She was one and a half and a bit. And she had only started talking. "Who are you?" were her first real words. But, because everybody who knew her loved her so much, they always knew exactly what she meant.

Here is what she actually said to the elf:

ELF: Get off me, please.

KAYLA: I'm very sorry.

VICTORIA: Bum-bum.

Oops. I forgot to explain about Victoria.

Victoria was the same age as Kayla, the exact same age. They were born at the exact same moment, in the same hospital, in the same ward, but not on the same bed. And now they lived next-door to each other. "Bum-bum" was or were Victoria's first word or words. But, because everybody who knew her loved her so much, they always knew exactly what *she* meant.

ELF: Get off me, please.

KAYLA: I'm very sorry.

VICTORIA: Ouch, me bum.

ELF: I'm too busy to answer that question.

KAYLA: Are you an elf?

VICTORIA: Are you an elf?

ELF: I told you. I'm too busy to answer.

KAYLA: Do you work for Santa?

VICTORIA: Are you spying on us?

ELF: Are you being cheeky? You'd better not be.

KAYLA: We've been really good.

VICTORIA: We'll stitch the dress back together again.

ELF: That does it. You're going into me book. What's your name?

KAYLA: Kayla.

VICTORIA: Victoria.

ELF: What's your name?

The elf took a pencil out from behind his very big ear. By the way, his other ear was very big too. So was his nose and both of his feet.

"Excuse me," said Jimmy.

"What?" said the elf.

"Stop being so grumpy."

And the elf kind of slumped.

"I'm sorry," he said. "It's just, I'm so busy."

"Who are you?" said Kayla.

"Yes," said the elf. "I do work for Santa."

He jumped, and pointed at Kayla.

"I understood her!"

"That's because you're not grumpy any more," said Robbie.

"Bum-bum," said Victoria.

"Thank you," said the elf.

A huge drop of rain fell from a branch and whacked the elf on the nose.

"Oh yes!" he said, as if he was waking up. "I'm looking for, for, for –"

He opened his notebook and flicked from page to page.

"For, for, for, for, for – oh yes. Rover. I'm looking for something called Rover."

"A dog?" said Jimmy.

The elf looked into the notebook again.

"A cat, a rat, a duck? Ah yes – a dog."

"He lives next door," said Robbie.

"Oh great, then I've found him."

"Why do you want him?" said Jimmy.

"I don't want him," said the elf. "The boss does. You see, Rudolph's gone on strike."

CHAPTER FOUR
WARNING:
WEAR GLOVES AND A HAT
WHEN YOU'RE READING THIS
CHAPTER BECAUSE IT TAKES
PLACE IN LAPLAND, IN THE
NORTH OF FINLAND, AND
IT'S VERY COLD THERE

"Please, Rudolph," said Santa.

"No, man," said Rudolph. "No can do."

They were in the barn behind Santa's house and workshop. Outside, elves on snowmobiles and sledges pulled by husky dogs charged across the yard. They were bringing sacks full of just-made presents to all the sleighs lined up in a long, long row. The reindeer were harnessed and very excited. This was their big night.

But, inside the barn, it was very quiet.

Santa was wearing a brand-new suit. It was red, of course, a beautiful bright red because it was so new. He had loved the old suit – the most famous suit in the world – but it had ripped when he was bending over to put on his boots.

"You need a new suit," said Mrs Claus as she looked at Santa's underpants sticking out of the big hole at the back of his trousers.

"I need a new bum," Santa laughed. "This one's too big."

But Santa wasn't laughing now. The suit was supposed to make anyone who wore it or saw it happy, but it wasn't working.

Santa looked sad, and worried. It was Christmas Eve. And time was flying. He had a sleigh full of presents and a cranky old reindeer who wouldn't pull it. He should have been in New Zealand by now, climbing down and back up chimneys. And then there was Australia, and Papua New Guinea and Borneo, the Philippines, Japan and then China. It was night-time in all those places, the end of Christmas Eve. Millions and millions of sleeping children, all of them waking up in a few hours. And what would they find?

Santa was very worried.

If the presents weren't there, that would be the end of it. No presents, no Santa. That was how it worked. All those kids, all over the world, would stop believing in him. The magic would die and Santa would just be a very old man, with nothing left to do.

Santa was terrified.

"Come on Rudi," he said. "We do it every year."

"No, man."

Rudolph was wearing his sunglasses and he had a bandanna tied around his antlers. (By the way, the bandanna had been given to him by a very old singer called Bruce Springsteen.)

"Oh, come on, Rudi," said Santa. "There are millions of children waiting for us. We have to give them their presents."

"But that's it, man," said Rudolph.

"That's all it's about these days. Presents, presents, presents. They're spoilt, man. The kids these days. They don't even say thanks."

"Yes, they do," said Santa.

"They don't mean it," said Rudolph.

"Don't be so cranky, Rudi," said Santa.

"Look, man, next year, maybe. It's a mid-life thing. I need a rest."

Rudolph lay down in the straw.

Santa patted him. Rudolph felt very hot and the world-famous nose was even redder than usual.

Santa knew.

"You have the flu, Rudi," said Santa.

"Sorry to let you down, man," said Rudolph.

"Don't worry," said Santa.

And Rudolph closed his eyes and slept. Santa put a blanket over his old friend's back. Then he went over to the sleigh. The presents were packed and ready, in sacks of different sizes. There were other sleighs already in the sky, all around the world, waiting to transfer more presents on to Santa's sleigh. All those children to be visited. All those countries, all those chimneys.

And here he was, stuck in the northern tip of Lapland, thousands of miles from where he should have been, on his way to New Zealand.

There were other reindeer. They were good, hard-working reindeer – but not good enough.

Rudolph was the strongest and the fastest. He was the best at reading the stars, at finding the way as he pulled the sleigh over the clouds. He was the best at parking on rooftops. He had the lightest hooves, the hooves of a ballet dancer. His hooves on slates never made a sound and they never went through straw roofs. And he sang all night as they flew from country to country. "Rudolph the coolest reindeer – you'll go down in his-TORY!"

Rudolph was the best.

But Rudolph was asleep and sick, and the famous nose looked like a tiny lighthouse in the middle of a very big ocean.

Santa patted Rudolph.

There was only one hope.

Santa knew what was what. He kept an eye on all the kids in the world, and their parents and pets. His elves sent reports to him. They wrote postcards, letters and e-mails. They sent carrier pigeons, Saint Bernard dogs and even an owl they borrowed from a kid called Potter. So, Santa knew: there was only one animal out there who could replace Rudolph. A dog. And that dog's name was – ROVER!!

CHAPTER FIVE
YOU CAN TAKE THE GLOVES OFF NOW, BUT LEAVE THE HAT ON BECAUSE IT'S STILL RAINING IN DUBLIN

ROVER!!

They looked at the dog asleep on his rug. The rug was in a shed behind the house. Rover's owners had put the rug there and left the shed door open so Rover would have somewhere to go when it was raining. It rains a lot in Ireland, so Rover had spent most of his life in the shed.

But that was fine with Rover.

Rover was fast, but so are a lot of dogs. He liked chasing things – cars, crows and helicopters – but so do most dogs. He pooed a lot, but so do all dogs. But what made Rover different was his mind. Rover had a brain the size of Africa tucked into a head the size of a baked potato. He pooed, yes, but then he sold the poo.

Does your dog do that?

Are you sure?

The fact is, very few dogs are brainy enough to sell their poo. But Rover sold his poo to the Gigglers, who then placed dollops of it on paths, to trap grown-ups who'd been mean to children. Rover also weed on the sides of cars, so that parents would pay their kids to wash the cars, and the kids always gave Rover ten per cent of the money. He'd been doing this for years and, like all dogs, he was a wee and poo factory. So Rover was a very rich dog.

Anyway, Rover was asleep on his rug. He loved lying on the rug because that was where he had his best ideas. It was a smelly old rug. It was so old, it was hardly there any more. In fact, the smell was the only solid bit of the rug left.

Rover snored.

"He's only pretending," said Jimmy. And Jimmy was right. Rover was pretending to be asleep.

THE RETURN OF
CHAPTER FOUR

Santa looked at the empty space in front of the sleigh, where Rudolph should have been.

He was getting more and more worried.

"What's keeping that elf?" he said to himself. "What's keeping that dog?"

He put his old head in his old hands. He was very cold and his back was beginning to hurt.

CHAPTER FIVE II

Rover kept his eyes shut.

When a gang of kids and an elf in a leather jacket called, looking excited and worried, that meant one of two things, trouble or work. And Rover wasn't in the mood for either of these things. He was a hard-working dog. But he was having a lazy day. He wasn't even scratching.

"Rover."

Rover's two eyes stayed shut.

"Bum-bum," said Victoria.

One of Rover's eyes opened.

"Rudolph's on strike? That's a pity."

And the eye closed again.

"But Santa wants you to pull the sleigh," said Robbie.

Rover's other eye opened.

"Do I look like a reindeer?"

The eye closed.

"Ah, come on, Rover."

"You can do it."

"Who are you?"

"Please, Rover."

"Bum-bum."

Rover knew: they weren't going to go away. His lazy day was vanishing in front of his closed eyes. Anyway, he liked kids. He hated to think that they wouldn't get their presents. And he'd always wanted to fly.

But Rover was a business dog.

"How much?" he said.

"Excuse me?" said the elf.

"How much will you pay me?"

"We were hoping you'd do it for nothing," said the elf.

"From the goodness of my heart?" said Rover. "That kind of thing?"

"Yes," said the elf.

Both of Rover's eyes opened.

"You want me to drag a sleigh full of presents and a fat lad in a red suit. And you want me to drag this sleigh all around the world? And you want me to do this for nothing?"

"Yes," said the elf.

The eyes closed, snap, like two smashed light bulbs.

"Night-night," said Rover. "Don't let the bugs bite."

And the elf took out his notebook.

CHAPTER FIVE'S BABY –
LITTLE CHAPTER SIX

"Let me sec, let me see," said the elf.
"Ah, yes."

He found the page he was looking for.

"I think," said the elf, "there's a girl dog in Galway called Lassie who'd be very interested in reading this."

One of Rover's eyes opened.

His girlfriend was called Lassie and she lived in Galway.

The elf continued.

"It says here," said the elf, "that a dog called Rover was seen holding paws with a girl dog *not* called Lassie when they went to see *My Dog Skip* at the Savoy last week."

Rover jumped up.

"When do we start?" he said.

"Good on yourself, Rover," said Robbie.

CHAPTER SIX –
THE TEENAGE YEARS

I don't want to be Chapter Six. I never asked to be Chapter Six. I'm not eating this muck. You don't understand my music. I want a car. Who said you could put my teddy bear up in the attic?

CHAPTER SEVEN

The elf closed his notebook with a happy snap.

"Let's get going," he said.

"Hold your horses, pal," said Rover. "If I go, I'll need help."

"What kind of help?" said the elf.

Rover pointed a paw at the children.

"That kind of help," he said.

"Great!" said Jimmy and Robbie, together.

"Children, delivering presents?" said the elf. "That's ridiculous."

"Listen, pal," said Rover. "Rover has one rule. In case of emergency, bring a child. This is a big emergency, right?"

"Right."

"Yeah. So, I'm bringing four children."

"But," said the elf.

"Great," said Rover. "I knew you'd see it my way. Right, kids," he said to Robbie, Jimmy, Kayla and Victoria. "Go home and get some warm clothes on."

The children ran.

"And, hey," said Rover. "Bring an atlas."

CHAPTER EIGHT

Robbie and Jimmy were dressed and ready.

Jimmy was wearing seven T-shirts, nine jumpers and four pairs of trousers.

Robbie was wearing nineteen T-shirts, three jumpers, a track-suit, three pairs of trousers and his bathing togs.

They were both wearing swimming goggles and *Liverpool* caps. They each had on a pair of their mother's mountaineering boots, stuffed full of slices of bread so they'd fit and stay warm.

And Robbie had his school atlas.

They were ready to go now, just waiting for Kayla.

They watched her coming down the stairs. Actually, she was sliding down the banister.

"Who are you?" she said, as she flew past them and hit the wall.

But she didn't hurt herself because she was wearing all the clothes she owned and some of her father's too. She had also made knee and elbow pads out of the nappies that she didn't need any more, because she had started using the potty.

She stood up and laughed.

They were ready to go.

Their mother, Billie-Jean Fleetwood
Mack, was upstairs in the attic,
practising her bungee-jumping.

"Mum!" called Robbie. "We're going
out!"

"Where to?" they heard their mother
say.

"Australia, Asia, Africa, Europe and
North and South America!"

Suddenly, their mother was right in
front of them, upside-down, her feet

tied to a rubber rope. She'd just jumped out of the attic.

"That sounds nice," she said.

She was wearing a magnificent gold crash helmet.

"Look after your brothers, won't you?" she said to Kayla.

"Who are you?"

"Good girl," said Dillie-Jean. "Have a nice time."

And she was gone, back into the attic. They heard her helmet whacking the inside of the roof.

"Oh-oh," she said. "There go two more slates. Your daddy won't be happy."

Robbie, Jimmy and Kayla ran out of the house.

CHAPTER NINE

Meanwhile, in the house next door, Victoria's mother was helping Victoria to zip up her padded jacket.

Her mother's name was Tina.

"Goodness," said Tina. "You must have grown since we last put this jacket on you. Yesterday."

Tina had a beautiful voice. Everybody said so. Even the birds stopped singing to listen to her. The toilet pipes stopped gurgling, the cooker stopped cooking, the fridge warmed up whenever they heard Tina's voice. She worked at a radio station. She presented a programme especially for people who lived in Ireland but hadn't been born there. The programme was called *Pawpaw and Potatoes.*

USEFUL INFORMATION

The pawpaw is a small fruit, found in most tropical countries, and the potato is a small animal, found in Ireland. All young Irish people learn how to hunt potatoes. And potatoes are easy to hunt because they don't have legs, so they can't run away, and they don't have mouths, so they can't beg for mercy. The best way to hunt potatoes is with a weapon called a potato peeler. Wild potatoes can be found hiding among the vegetables in supermarkets. They can also be found in kitchens, where they nest in plastic bags, often in the bottom of fridges.

WARNING!

Organic potatoes are particularly dangerous. Be very careful when approaching them. And don't try hunting other wild animals, like lions and crocodiles, with a potato peeler.

Now, back to the story.

The programme was called *Pawpaw and Potatoes*. It was very popular. Everybody listened to it. Not just people who hadn't been born in Ireland. People who'd been born in Ireland listened too. People who had never been outside Ireland, not even for five minutes in a boat, not even for ten seconds for a swim – even these people listened to *Pawpaw and Potatoes*. Because they loved Tina's voice.

What was it like?

Her voice was like silk.

Silk doesn't have a voice.

Shut up! Her voice was like silk. It was like ice cream. It was like hot fudge. (A note for the adults: it was like a really good pint of Guinness.) It was like gravy. It was like the most beautiful music. It was like a baby laughing, like Bambi belching. Like a butterfly whispering, like a peacock farting. It was the beautiful voice of a beautiful woman, that was what it was. Does that answer your question?

Kind of.

Anyway, Tina had been looking everywhere for her best dress.

She zipped up Victoria's jacket and stood up.

"Did you see my best dress anywhere, Vicki-baa?"

"Bum-bum."

And Tina started laughing.

"You made a parachute with it?"

And she hugged Victoria and kissed the top of her head.

"Where do you get these ideas from?"

The telly turned itself on and off. It was showing off for Tina.

"Now," said Tina. "Have a nice time with Kayla. And don't go too far without asking permission first."

"Bum-bum?"

And Tina laughed again.

"Yes," she said. "You *may* go to Vietnam."

The telly changed channels and put the picture upside-down.

Victoria galloped through the kitchen to the back door.

"Hey, young one," said the cooker. "Is your ma coming in?"

"Bum-bum," said Victoria.

And she ran out of the door.

"Hey, lads," said the cooker. "Tina's coming!"

"Oh goodie," said the toaster.

"Is my hair OK?" said the fridge.

CHAPTER TEN

Meanwhile, Santa sat on a big log outside the reindeer's barn. He took his old head from his hands and looked up at the stars.

"Where are they?" he said.

CHAPTER ELEVEN

They were in Rover's garden.

The elf and Rover, Victoria and Kayla, Jimmy and Robbie. They were holding hands and paws in Rover's garden.

And, suddenly, they weren't. They weren't there any more.

They were standing beside Santa, up to their knees in snow.

How did that happen?

CHAPTER TWELVE

I'm not telling.
It's a secret.

CHAPTER THIRTEEN

Santa fell off the log.

But he jumped up again when he saw who had arrived.

"Boy, oh, girl," he said. "It's good to see you lot."

And then he did it. He gave his famous laugh.

"Ho ho ho!"

He hadn't laughed all day, but now his belly shook. It was the nicest, funniest sound they'd ever heard. His laugh made them laugh, and that made him laugh again, louder.

"HO ho ho!"

And he looked at Rover.

"The famous Rover," he said.

"The famous Santa," said Rover. "Where's the famous sleigh?"

"Inside the famous barn," said Santa.

And he looked at all the children.

"Who have we here?" he said.

"Four kids," said Robbie.

"So I see," said Santa.

"And an elf," said Jimmy.

"Who are you?" said Kayla.

"Nice to meet you, Kayla," said Santa.

"He brought them, Santa," said the elf, pointing at Rover. "It had nothing to do with me."

"The more the merrier," said Santa. "We need children tonight."

"Sorry to butt in here, lads," said

Rover. "But we have a sleigh here, a
lot of presents, a lot of kids and not a
lot of time."

He looked at Santa.

"So, big man," he said. "Why don't
you hitch me up and we can hit
the sky."

"Do you think you can do it?"said
Santa.

"No sweat," said Rover. "The
name's Bond. Rover Bond."

Santa put the blue harness over
Rover's back.

"Is that too tight, Rover?"

"If it was too tight, pal, you'd know all about it. Are we ready to roll?"

The children climbed on to the sleigh.

"Is that Rudolph?" said Jimmy.

Rudolph was still asleep on the straw.

"He's having the night off," said Santa.

"He only works one night a year," said Rover. "But who's complaining? Are we ready?"

Rudolph opened his eyes.

"A dog pulling my sleigh!" he said. "Oh man, I'm going out of my mind!"

Santa covered Rudolph again, and patted his fur until he went back to sleep. Then he went over to Rover.

"Rover," he said.

"I'm listening," said Rover.

Santa spoke very quietly, so the children wouldn't hear him.

"I don't think we can do it," he said.

"Trust me," said Rover.

"I do trust you," said Santa. "It's not the speed. It's the chimneys, the bedrooms, the tricky stuff. I don't think we have the time."

"Guess what I have," said Rover.

"What?" said Santa.

"An idea," said Rover.

And that was how the lizards came back into the story.

CHAPTER FOURTEEN
THIS CHAPTER IS DEDICATED TO LIZARDS EVERYWHERE

Heidi kissed Hans's forehead.

"Thanks for the fly, Hans."

"Thanks for eating it, Heidi."

They were under the wet bush in the Macks' back garden.

And, suddenly, they weren't. The bush and the garden were gone and they were in Santa's barn.

How did that happen?

The answer is in the next chapter, on Page 70. Have a look. We'll wait for you.

They landed and bounced, and landed again.

"Wow," said Hans.

Then he saw Rover.

"Hi-dee-hi, Rover."

"Cold enough for you?" said Rover.

And Hans and Heidi suddenly noticed. It was cold. It was very cold.

How cold?

Did you ever stick your head in a freezer for ten minutes?

No.

Why not?

It's too cold.

Well, that was how cold it was. And Hans loved it.

"Nice," he said. "Very nice."

He rubbed his tummy on the ground.

"Very, very nice."

"Want to go where it gets even colder?" said Rover. "And help save Christmas at the same time?"

"Sounds cold," said Heidi.

"Sounds great," said Hans.

"Hop on board," said Rover.

"Okey-dokey, Rovie."

And Hans and Heidi jumped on to the sleigh. They landed on Victoria's lap, then hopped to the floor.

"Hi-dee-hi, kids."

"Bum-bum."

"Now," said Rover. "Let's break out of this place."

Santa stood up in the sleigh. He held the reins. He laughed – "Ho ho ho" – and shouted.

"Hey, ho! And away we go!"

And away they went.

Out of the barn door, into the yard, across the snow and up, pulled by the mighty Rover.

Up, up, up, and away. Into the air, into the sky. The elf waved goodbye.

Hang on.

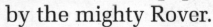

Yes?

I know that reindeer can fly some-times, but what about Rover? I've never seen a flying dog. Except for the one who was running after the plane and bit the wheel just when the plane was taking off. But what about Rover? He can't fly, can he?

Nine times out of ten, ninety-nine times out of a hundred, dogs can't fly. Take your dog to the park and say, "Bonzo, fly!" Bonzo will probably sit there and look back at you with one of those faces that says, "Sorry, chum, I'll chase your ball, I'll fetch your stick, I'll eat your shoe, I'll lick your granny's bald head, but I'm not going to be flying today." So, fair enough, dogs can't fly. But, *but*, BUT – when you're hanging around with Santa, you can expect magic things to happen, and that was exactly what was happening now. Magic. And good magic can never be explained.

Because it's magic. The real thing. Santa magic. Once-a-year magic. But, *but*, BUT – here's a 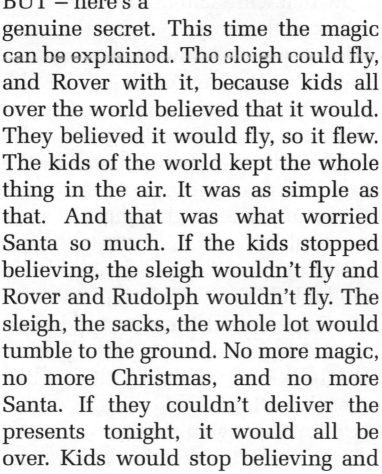 genuine secret. This time the magic can be explained. The sleigh could fly, and Rover with it, because kids all over the world believed that it would. They believed it would fly, so it flew. The kids of the world kept the whole thing in the air. It was as simple as that. And that was what worried Santa so much. If the kids stopped believing, the sleigh wouldn't fly and Rover and Rudolph wouldn't fly. The sleigh, the sacks, the whole lot would tumble to the ground. No more magic, no more Christmas, and no more Santa. If they couldn't deliver the presents tonight, it would all be over. Kids would stop believing and

Christmas Day would become just another day of the year, a day off school, a day off work – nothing more. Rover was pulling more than a sleigh full of presents. He was pulling the future of Christmas. But he didn't know that. Only Santa knew.

Back to the story.

Rover didn't know how come he could fly. But he knew he would. When he jumped, when he felt his paws climbing the air like it was solid and friendly, he knew he was in the magic hands of Santa.

"I'm impressed!" he shouted over his shoulder.

"Nothing to it!" Santa shouted back. "Ho ho ho!"

Santa was glad there were kids on board. They made up for the loss of Rudolph. Rover flew beautifully, like an eagle with invisible wings.

Up, up they went.

They saw the world below, the

shining snow of northern Finland, the farmhouses, the lights from the kitchen windows lighting the snow.

Up, and away.

They saw snow-coated trees and the lights from the Spar supermarket in a small town called Muonio.

Up, up, up.

They saw the lights of Helsinki, the biggest city in Finland. And blocks of ice shining like giant, rolling diamonds in the Gulf of Finland. Up, up, into the clouds, and up.

CHAPTER FIFTEEN

Ha ha.
Fooled you.
It's a secret.

CHAPTER SIXTEEN

Up through the clouds they went.

"Ho ho ho."

And Rover picked up speed. They all hung on to the sleigh. They saw stars – millions of them – for a second, and then they were in clouds again. Then stars, more clouds, and stars, and nothing but stars. Glorious, beautiful, dancing, shooting stars. And others that stayed still and didn't shoot or dance at all.

And these were the stars that Robbie and Jimmy looked up at. These stars were their map, now that the land below was hidden by the clouds.

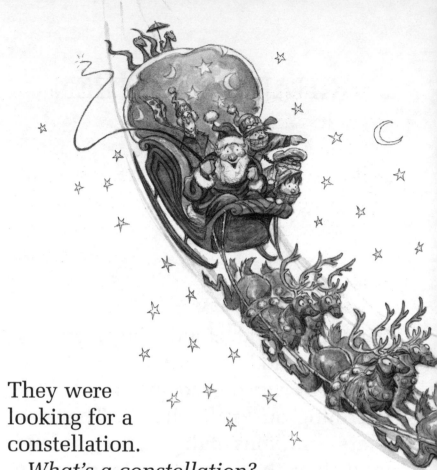

They were
looking for a
constellation.

What's a constellation?

Good question. A constellation
is a group of stars. For thousands of
years, people have been able to find
their way in the dark by following
these stars. The most famous constellation is probably the Plough. The
Plough is seven stars that look like an
old-fashioned plough.

"Look!" said Robbie.

He'd found the constellation they were looking for.

"The Teacher's Armpit," said Jimmy.

It was, indeed, the Teacher's Armpit. Thirty-seven stars that are shaped like a teacher's armpit. Seven stars make up the armpit and the other thirty make up the hair.

"Which way, lads?" Rover shouted back, over his shoulder.

"Follow that armpit, Rover," shouted Robbie. "South-east."

And that's where Rover brought

them, through the freezing sky over Estonia and Russia. His paws gripped the air like it was solid ground. He pulled them south, back into daytime. The stars disappeared and so did the clouds. Over the Caspian Sea and Iran. His snout cut through the air like it was warm butter. Over Pakistan and India.

They headed south. And they also flew east. They were over clouds again, so they couldn't see the countries and oceans below them. And then they couldn't see the clouds because Rover had pulled them into the night.

It was nine hours later, even though it was only twenty minutes since they'd flown out of the barn.

Jimmy and Robbie and Kayla and Victoria looked up for the next constellation.

Santa looked at his watch.

"Ho ho ho – I hope."

CHAPTER SIX –
THE ADULT

I hope they're wrapped up warm. I hope they're wearing their safety belts. I hope they have some sandwiches in case they get hungry on the way. I hope they remember their phone numbers in case they get lost. I hope they don't make too much noise when they're going over our house.

CHAPTER SEVENTEEN
THIS CHAPTER IS DEDICATED
TO ALL THE FLIES THAT
HAVE BEEN EATEN BY
LIZARDS EVERYWHERE

And then they saw it.

"Who are you?"

They all spotted it at the same time, the second most famous constellation of them all.

"The Monkey's Bum!" said Robbie.

Forty-three stars shining happily. Twenty-four made up the bum and the other nineteen made up his underpants.

And the Monkey's Bum pointed them at New Zealand.

How?

Here was the trick. You had to look straight at it, for ten seconds without blinking. You had to stay absolutely still. So Rover stopped flying.

And they all stared.

For ten seconds.

Ten.

Seconds.

Ten.

Lo-ong.

Seconds.

And then it did it. The Monkey's Bum wriggled and did a little dance. Then stopped, pointing the way.

And they were off again.

"Follow that bum!"

"Hey ho, and away we go!"

South and east. Fast, fast, fast. Over the Indian Ocean, Thailand and Borneo. Faster than the fastest horse, the fastest car or snail, faster than the speed of sound and light, Rover dragged them over Papua New Guinea.

And down, through the clouds they went, as they flew over the Coral Sea. They could see ship lights on the ocean. Down, down, because soon they would be landing.

Soon the real work was going to start.

CHAPTER SIX

We didn't have silly chapters like this when I was young. We had proper stories. And we didn't have pictures either. Where did I leave my teeth? And we didn't have televisions. Or food. Oh, there are my teeth. Biting my leg. Now, how did they get there?

I like the dog though. And the children. And Santa, of course. Come to think of it, I did have a book with pictures. I had lots of books with pictures. And four tellys. And we did have food once. Now, where have they gone? Biting my other leg. I remember the days when teeth knew their place. In your mouth. That was where teeth went when I was young.

CHAPTER EIGHTEEN

And now they could see the lights of Auckland, the biggest city in New Zealand.

"Action stations, lads and lassies," said Santa. "Now, where's my list?"

Santa held on to Rover's reins with one hand and searched inside his red jacket and gave himself a good old scratch while he was at it.

"Where, where, where, where?"

"Where do we start, Santa?" said Jimmy.

"I don't know," said Santa.

He sounded worried.

"I can't remember."

And the sleigh started tumbling out of the sky.

CHAPTER NINETEEN

They all held on as the sleigh fell.
They heard Rover but they couldn't
see him.

"Who stole me wings!?"

He was under the sleigh.

The sleigh began to spin as it fell.

Santa knew what was happening.
When he'd said, "I don't know," the
kids had begun to wonder if he was
the real Santa. The real Santa would

never have said something like that. That was what they thought. But Santa was hopeless at stars and streets. He always had been. The stars and streets were Rudolph's department. Santa had a list of all the streets but he couldn't find it. And now the ocean was getting nearer and nearer as the sleigh continued to fall.

But he found it. Deep in his inside pocket – the kids were screaming and so were the lizards – he found the paper and pulled. And the kids saw the longest list they'd ever seen, a piece of paper that flapped in the wind and flew behind and above them like a tail.

And that was enough. They believed again – it was a Santa kind of list – and the sleigh and Rover stopped spinning and falling and the air stopped rushing past them. Rover could feel the air, like solid ground, under his paws again.

"No more messing," he said, over his shoulder. "We've got work to do."

"It's all the streets in alphabetical order," Santa told the kids as the sleigh dropped nice and slowly to the moonlit roofs of Auckland. "With all the children in each house. Abacus Street, Rover," he shouted to Rover. "I remember now. The second left after the lights down there. Pull up at the first roof, Rover."

Rover turned left on to the long, tree-lined street and, as if he'd been pulling and parking sleighs all his life, he brought the sleigh over to the first roof and dropped and slid and quietly, quietly stopped it on the slates. Not a scratch or a scrape or a bump.

"Nothing to it," whispered Rover.

Santa climbed out of the sleigh.

"Oh, my poor legs are stiff. Notice how warm it is?" he said.

"Who are you?" said Kayla.

"That's right," said Santa. "It's

summer down here. But keep all your clothes on in case you fall off a roof. Right," he said. "Let's get going."

And this was where the children, after years and years of getting presents from Santa, got the chance to pay him back.

DEAD
CHAPTER SIX

Hello!

It's nice up here.

Guess what I can see out of my window?

A big monkey's bum.

CHAPTER TWENTY
THIS CHAPTER IS DEDICATED TO NOBODY BECAUSE WE'RE IN A BIT OF A HURRY

Kayla lifted one of her jumpers and showed them what she'd hidden under it. Two of her mother's rubber bungee-jumping ropes, wrapped round and round her tummy. She started to unroll them.

"Who are you?" she said.

"Another brilliant idea from Kayla," said Jimmy.

They grabbed a rope and pulled. Kayla spun like a spinning top. She went whizzing to the edge of the roof but Santa caught her just in time.

"Who are you?"

"You're welcome," said Santa. "Now show me your idea."

Kayla tied one end of a rubber rope round her waist and handed the other end to Robbie.

"She needs the presents for this house," said Robbie.

Santa took five parcels from a sack and handed them to Kayla.

And then she jumped down the chimney.

Santa knew a good idea when he saw one.

"Ho ho ho," he laughed, very quietly. Robbie was holding on to the rope. He felt it tighten.

"Here she comes," he said, and a second later Kayla flew feet-first out of the chimney, and landed on Robbie's shoulders. She'd left the parcels down inside the house.

Meanwhile, Victoria tied one end of the second rope around her waist and Jimmy held the other end. Santa sorted out the parcels and began to feel very happy. But then –

"Oh, no," he said. "I forgot a parcel. Blocks for the baby."

"No problem," said Rover. "Right, lads," he said to the lizards. "Get down off the sleigh and show the man your stuff."

Hans and Heidi jumped on to the roof.

"It's getting crowded up here," said Jimmy.

Hans dropped his tummy to the roof.

"Hot," he said. "I think I'll change my name back to Omar."

And, immediately, the heat in the slates began to feel wonderful.

Omar spoke to Santa.

"Mister Claus. Do you remember, by any chance, do they get the presents under the tree or at the end of the bed in this house?"

"End of the bed," said Santa.

"And where's the babby's bed?" said Omar.

"Down the hall, first door after the toilet."

"Okey-dokey. Now, Mister Claus, could you please put the parcel on to the end of my tongue."

And, suddenly, Omar's tongue was right in front of Santa's nose. He held the parcel out and it stuck to the tongue like a stamp to a letter.

Omar jumped on to the chimney pot. And he fired his tongue down the chimney, down the hall, past the toilet, into the baby's bedroom. He wriggled his tongue, and the parcel fell off, neatly on to the end of the cot.

When his tongue came back up it held a plate with cheese sandwiches on it. And, suddenly, the plate was under Santa's nose.

"For you," said Omar.

And while Santa ate the sandwiches – but not the crusts – Rover brought the children and the lizards from roof to roof along Abacus Street. The street was done, all the presents delivered, before Santa had finished chewing the second sandwich.

CHAPTER TWENTY-ONE
THIS CHAPTER IS
DEDICATED TO KILLER
POTATOES EVERYWHERE

Blackhead Street.

Chlorine Street.

Dolphin Avenue.

Eagle Street.

They delivered the presents to every home in Auckland. And then they flew on to Christchurch and delivered to all the homes along the way. Omar and Heidi were able to flick their tongues down chimneys while the sleigh was moving and high above the chimneys.

By the way, Heidi's warm name was Sunshine.

Fluffy Street.

Gasp Street.

Hardware Avenue.

They were finished with Christchurch and all of New Zealand before

Santa had finished his three hundred and fifty-second sandwich.

"Where now?" said Rover. "Australia?"

"Nope," said Santa, and he sprayed breadcrumbs and little cheese bits into the sky. "Head north first, Rover. We have to beat the sun."

And as he said it, they could see the very tip of the sun, not even the tip – the light that was coming from the tip – rising, slowly, slowly, but rising steadily out of the ocean far away to the east.

"Oh oh," said Robbie.

"No problem," said Rover.

And up they flew – up, up and north.

CHAPTER TWENTY-TWO
THIS CHAPTER IS DEDICATED TO FLYING DOGS EVERYWHERE.

As they went north they stopped at every island on the way.

Norfolk Island.

New Guinea.

Guam.

And they parked on every roof that could take the weight of the sleigh.

When the roofs were made of straw Rover parked beside the house and Santa and the kids climbed in a window.

Every time they flew back into the sky there was another sleigh waiting for them, with full sacks to replace the ones they'd emptied. Rover didn't stop or slow down. The new sleigh flew beside him until the elves had thrown the new sacks on to the back of Santa's sleigh.

But the reindeer pulling the other sleighs couldn't keep up with Rover, not even the youngest reindeer, Nasu.

USEFUL INFORMATION

Nasu is the Finnish word for "Piglet". And, while we're at it, *Nalle Puh* are the Finnish words for "Pooh Bear", and *kakki* is the Finnish word for "poo". Lesson over, back to the story.

The children looked back and waved at the puffing reindeer as Rover charged north in his race against the sun – over forests and deserts, giant lakes and football pitches.

Slowly, slowly, the sun was creeping up out of the ocean, a tiny bit more every time Santa looked.

So he didn't look.

They flew to the far north of Siberia, and Rover ran on the spot so his paws wouldn't get frozen to the roofs.

And then they were heading south again.

Korea, North.

Korea, South.

Korea, in the middle.

Rover nearly crashed in Hong Kong. They flew down into fog and, suddenly, there was a glass skyscraper right in front of him, a few feet from his nose. He took a sharp turn left, and the side of the sleigh whacked the wall but didn't break the glass.

"Stupid place to put a building," said Rover.

The Philippines.

East Timor.

Australia took a bit longer than Japan. There were two reasons for this. First, it's bigger. Second, they were attacked by a flock of birds with machine guns.

A VERY ANNOYING COMMERCIAL BREAK

BRUSH YOUR TEETH WITH DENTOFRESH TOOTHPASTE.

FAMOUS FOOTBALLERS BRUSH THEIR TEETH WITH NEW, IMPROVED DENTOFRESH.

DENTOFRESH – BRUSH YOUR TEETH WITH IT AND GIRLS WILL THINK YOU'RE COOL.

DENTOFRESH – BRUSH YOUR TEETH WITH IT AND BOYS WILL THINK YOU'RE COOL.

And now, back to the story.

CHAPTER TWENTY-THREE
THIS CHAPTER IS DEDICATED TO PEOPLE WHO USE DENTOFRESH EVERYWHERE

Jalopy Street.

Kangaroo Street.

They sat on a rooftop at the end of Lambchop Avenue, waiting for Santa for come up out of the last chimney. Rover's back was covered in snow, even though it was the middle of summer in Melbourne. It was the snow that had dropped on him in Siberia, thousands of miles away.

They were eating some of Santa's sandwiches, when they heard a voice behind them.

"Hands up."

They all turned.

It was a bird that was talking and he was pointing a machine gun at them. There were six other birds with him, all pointing machine guns at Robbie, Jimmy, Kayla, Victoria and Rover.

They were tall and orange, with red feathers standing up and waving on their heads. Their legs were pink, their claws were navy blue.

"Who are you?" said Kayla.

"We're the boorakooka birds," said the leader.

"That's us," said his friends.

"You didn't laugh," said the bird leader. "People used to laugh, every time we said boorakooka. Until we got the machine guns. Hand over the sack."

"No," said Jimmy.

"I have a machine gun. You don't have a machine gun. Hand over the sack."

"No," said Robbie.

"Hand it over."

"Bum-bum."

"It is *not* plastic," said the leader.

"Yes, it is."

"No, it isn't."

"Bruce!"

Santa's head was sticking out of the chimney.

The leader tried to hide the machine gun behind his back.

Santa climbed out of the chimney.

"I'm disappointed, Bruce," he said. "You said in your letter that you'd never point the machine gun at anybody."

"What machine gun?" said Bruce.

"Yeah," said the others. "What machine guns?"

"The ones behind your backs," said Santa. "Sticking up over your shoulders."

"They're only plastic, Santa," said Bruce.

"I know that, Bruce," said Santa. "I'd never give anyone a real machine gun for Christmas. But it's rude to point them."

"Sorry, Santa."

"That's OK, Bruce. Now, lads," he said to the boorakooka birds. "Go home to your nests and be asleep by the time I get there, or there'll be nothing for you this year."

And the boorakooka birds were gone. Just a few feathers floating in the air, that was all that was left of them. And, as Rover pulled the sleigh up to the sky, Santa leaned out – Robbie and Jimmy held him by his belt – and dropped presents into the boorakooka nests, in a huge eucalyptus gum tree at the end of Lambchop Avenue. They could see the machine guns hanging from the branches like Christmas decorations and, as they flew higher and higher, they could still hear the boorakooka birds snoring.

ANOTHER
COMMERCIAL BREAK

★ ★ ★ ★ ★ ★ ★ ★ ★

DO YOUR MAD COWS
HAVE BAD BREATH?

BRUSH THEIR TEETH WITH
FRESH-BREATH DENTOFRESH
IN THE NEW, IMPROVED TUBE.

★ ★ ★ ★ ★ ★ ★ ★ ★

CHAPTER TWENTY-FOUR

They went north, and back down south, and north again, and south. Like wipers on a rainy windscreen they swept across the world, with the sun always right behind them, getting a tiny bit nearer every time they looked.

Santa could feel the sun tickling the back of his neck, but it didn't make him laugh. It just made him more and more worried.

Bangladesh, all of Russia, Uzbekistan.

It was night-time in front of them and morning behind.

Iran, Oman, Libya.

Omar went back to Hans and back to Omar.

Finland, Bulgaria, Chad.

Sunshine went back to Heidi and back to Sunshine.

They saw lion packs asleep and packs of people coming home from parties.

Cameroon, Italy, Sweden.

They saw milkmen delivering milk and mad cows with bad breath dancing in the moonlight.

And when they came to Lagos, the biggest city in Nigeria, Victoria found the house of her grandparents.

THE BATTLE OF
THE PASTE

★ ★ ★ ★ ★ ★ ★ ★

BRUSH YOUR TEETH WITH
NEW TOOTHOFRESH AND
GIRLS WILL THINK YOU'RE
MUCH COOLER THAN
THEY DID WHEN YOU
USED DENTO-YUCKY-FRESH.

★ ★ ★ ★ ★ ★ ★ ★

CHAPTER
TWENTY-FIVE

Victoria had never seen her grand-parents' house before but it was easy to spot from the sleigh.

When she was a little girl, Victoria's mother, Tina, had climbed up on to the roof of the Mama and the Papa's house with a tin of paint and a big paintbrush. And she had painted this message in enormous letters:

Even after twenty years, the message was still loud and clear on the roof.

Her mother had told her so much about the house that Victoria had a perfect picture of it in her head – the blue windows, the red tin roof – and there it was now, right below her.

Rover swooshed down out of the sky over Lagos and landed on his velvet paws right beside the chimney. Jimmy held the bungee rope and Victoria jumped.

She landed in the big fireplace in the kitchen. Then she crept to the Mama and the Papa's bed. She had never seen them before, only in photographs. They were asleep and dreaming. She could tell: their dreams were sad. All of their children lived far away from Nigeria and they had never held and cuddled any of their grandchildren. Their dreams were full of empty rooms and voices belonging to children they couldn't see.

Victoria took two snow-domes out

of her jacket pocket. A snow-dome is a little glass dome full of water and thousands and thousands of plastic snowflakes. These were Dublin snow-domes. When you shook them the snow fell on to the River Liffey and the cacti that line the streets beside the river, and on to a sign that said, A PRESENT FROM DUBLIN.

Victoria put one dome under the Papa's pillow and the other one under the Mama's. She kissed them on their foreheads.

Then she crept back to the fireplace and pulled the rope.

ANOTHER
COMMERCIAL BREAK

★ ★ ★ ★ ★ ★ ★ ★

ONLY EEJITS USE
TOOTHOFRESH –

BRUSH YOUR TEETH
WITH CLINICALLY PROVEN
DENTOFRESH.

★ ★ ★ ★ ★ ★ ★ ★

CHAPTER TWENTY-SIX

Above the clouds over Dublin, they met the sleigh that carried the Dublin presents, pulled by a reindeer called Paddy Last. They caught all the sacks that the elves threw at them.

Then Santa's sleigh came out of the clouds and they saw Dublin Bay below them. They all cheered. They were nearly home. They could see the city getting bigger and bigger.

But, suddenly, Robbie was worried. And, at the exact same time, Jimmy was worried.

"Hey, Santa," said Robbie.

"Ho ho ho," said Santa.

"We're not finished yet, are we?"

"No, no, no," said Santa. "We've all of Ireland, Iceland, Greenland, some other islands, and all the countries of North America, Central America and South America. And Hawaii."

"But," said Jimmy. "When we're in America, our parents will wake up because it will be morning here. Right?"

"Right," said Santa.

"And they'll see that we're not here," said Robbie. "And they'll be worried sick."

"And we'll be in trouble when we get home," said Jimmy.

"I never thought of that," said Santa.

"What'll we do?"

"I don't know," said Santa. "I really don't know."

The sleigh wobbled and began to tumble.

"Who are you?" said Kayla.

"Yes!" said Santa. "Great idea, Kayla." And it was a great idea. Santa made the Mack parents and Victoria's parents sleep much longer than usual.

How?

Not telling.

The children landed on their own roofs and, while their parents slept, Victoria, Robbie, Jimmy and Kayla went down their own chimneys, and delivered their own presents to themselves. Robbie delivered Jimmy's and Jimmy delivered Robbie's.

"What did I get?" said Robbie.

"Not telling you," said Jimmy. "It's a surprise, ha ha. What did I get?"

"A doll, a drum, a kick in the bum and a chase around the table," said Robbie, "ha ha."

"Is Tina up yet?" said the toaster as Victoria sneaked through the kitchen.

"Does this shirt match my jacket?" said the fridge.

In only six minutes they were

finished with Dublin, and seven minutes later they'd done the rest of Ireland and they were flying out over the Atlantic Ocean, north towards Iceland. And while their children rode through a storm, their parents had the nicest dreams they'd ever had and slept through most of Christmas Day. Tina dreamed that she saw the Mama and the Papa lying in bed, at home in Lagos. They had big smiles on their sleeping faces. And Mister Mack dreamed about big, sexy cream crackers.

"My best-before date is the twentieth of October, 2004. Isn't that interesting?"

"I contain wheat flour, vegetable oil, salt and yeast. Isn't that interesting?"

And hundreds of miles away, Rover pushed into the storm.

"I wouldn't put a dog out in this weather," he muttered to himself.

"Ho ho ho," said Santa.

He looked behind him.

The sun was creeping up on them. Santa could put adults to sleep, but that kind of magic didn't work on the sun.

"Ho ho ho," said Santa.

CHAPTER
TWENTY-SEVEN

Meanwhile, back in Lagos, the sun poked a finger through a gap in the curtains and woke the Papa and the Mama. They sat up together. They were feeling happy for the first time in years and years.

The Papa put his hand up to his forehead. He'd had a dream that his little granddaughter had kissed him, and now he could feel it, the kiss – it was still wet there in the middle of his forehead. (And it stayed there, wet and wonderful, for the rest of his long life.) And the Mama felt the kiss on her forehead too. She touched it, and cried happy tears. (And the kiss stayed there, a lovely tickle, for the rest of her long life, and even after.)

They looked at each other.

"Did you dream what I dreamed?" said the Mama.

"I think so," said the Papa.

And he felt something under his pillow. The snow-dome. He took it out and shook it and watched the snow falling on Dublin. And the Mama found her dome and shook it, too.

They held hands as they shook their domes.

"Dublin looks like a nice place," said the Papa.

"Yes," said the Mama. "Look, the air is full of sugar."

DENTOFRESH IS LOW IN
FLUORIDE AND SUGAR-FREE.
IT PROTECTS YOUR TEETH
AGAINST TOOTH DECAY.
ISN'T THAT INTERESTING?

IF YOU BRUSH YOUR TEETH
WITH TOOTHOFRESH, YOUR
TEETH WILL FALL OUT
AND YOU WILL DIE.
ISN'T THAT INTERESTING?

CHAPTER TWENTY-EIGHT
THIS CHAPTER IS DEDICATED TO SNOW-DOMES EVERYWHERE

Iceland, Greenland, Newfoundland.

They flew down the east coast of Canada, the U.S.A., across the sea to the Bahamas, Cuba and Jamaica. They hopped from island to island, dropping presents down chimneys and through open windows where there were no chimneys.

Brazil, Uruguay, Argentina.

In twenty-two minutes they delivered more than twenty million pairs of football boots to football-crazy kids. They went to the very tip of Argentina, to Tierra del Fuego, to the very last house before the South Pole.

And they flew back north, through the centre of South America.

Paraguay, Bolivia, Colombia.

The sun was crawling towards them. But they kept going, in the last minutes and seconds of darkness. Back up to the U.S.A.

New Mexico, Colorado, Wyoming.

The sun was beginning to light the snow on the Rocky Mountains, but they kept diving down and up the chimneys.

Alaska, the Yukon, British Columbia.

They flew south again, along the west coast of the Americas. And the sun peeked over the mountains. Suddenly, it was early morning.

"Please!" Santa roared at the sun. "Just give us five minutes!"

But the sun wasn't listening. Because the sun has no ears. Anyway, the sun wasn't moving – Earth was. But Earth doesn't have ears either, so Santa was wasting his time. And he knew. It was too late.

He let go of the reins and put his old head in his hands. He wasn't Santa any more. Because he'd failed. There were millions of kids who still hadn't got their presents, and they wouldn't be getting them now because they'd be waking up. And what would they find? Nothing. Nothing at the end of their beds, nothing under the Christmas tree. Santa had let them down. He was just a useless old man with nothing left to do. He waited for the sleigh to tumble out of the sky.

But it didn't.

It stayed up there.

Rover wasn't running, so they weren't moving. But they definitely weren't falling. Santa looked over the side of the sleigh, to check.

"What's wrong, Santa?" said Jimmy.

"Oh, kids, I'm sorry," said Santa.

"Why?" said Robbie.

"I'm not going to deliver the presents. All those poor children. They won't believe in me any more."

"Yes, they will," said Jimmy.

"Bum-bum."

"It's *you* we like, Santa," said Robbie. "The presents are just extra."

"Yeah," said Jimmy. "And, anyway, we already got our presents, so we don't care that much."

And the others nodded, even Hans and Heidi.

Rover had unhitched himself and he now climbed into the sleigh.

"Is this a private conversation, or can any dog join in?" he said.

"What do you think, Rover?" said Santa.

"About what, exactly?" said Rover.

"About not delivering the rest of the presents."

"Who says we won't?" said Rover.

"But it's too late," said Santa. "They won't believe in me any more."

He pointed at the sun.

"I don't get it," said Rover. "One of the kids down there wants a doll. Is it a better doll because you deliver it in the dark?"

"Well. No."

"So, what's the problem?" said Rover. "Give the poor kid her doll."

"In daylight? Now?"

"I'm not hanging around till night-time, pal," said Rover. "Think about it. All those kids wake up. Boo-hoo. No presents. Then you fall down the chimney with the presents. And you're worried that they won't believe in you? Cop on."

Nobody said anything for a while, then –

"Ho ho ho," said Santa.

"Now you're talking," said Rover.

THE RETURN OF DEAD
CHAPTER SIX

Guess what I just saw flying past my window?

A dog pulling a sleigh full of kiddies and lizards.

Ooh, I like it up here.

Hey, Elvis, come over here and look at this.

CHAPTER
TWENTY-NINE

They made it.

Every house and hut and flat and apartment and trailer and caravan and hospital and igloo – every home and building that had a child in it – they delivered the presents to them all. Kids laughed and grown-ups fainted when Santa fell down the chimney.

They were nearly stopped in Mexico, when they met the Walking Poo of Guadalajara. This was a huge poo that stood on people, getting them back for all the poos that people stand on every day. But, just in time, they saw the giant yucky foot coming down on them, and they legged it, back to the sleigh, and up and away.

"Come back here, *amigos*, till I stomp on yis," yelled the Walking Poo.

"Happy Christmas, Poo!" they yelled back as they flew on to Mexico City.

And they were nearly stopped when Rover crashed in Honolulu. He saw a lovely-looking collie below them and he watched her as she sniffed a gate. And he kept watching as he flew past – straight into a huge palm tree.

"Who put that there?" said Rover as they fell through the branches, to the ground.

They weren't hurt.

"Sorry, lads," said Rover.

"You were blinded by love, Rovie," said Hans.

"If you say so, pal," said Rover.

Kayla and Victoria fixed the sleigh.

How?

They put the runners back on it.

How?

With super-glue.

What super-glue?

Shut up.

And they were up and away again.

To Samoa, Phoenix Island and the very last stop, Midway Island.

To the last house.

On the very end of the very last street.

Number 27, Zulu Street.

They stood back and let Santa climb down the last chimney.

BATTLE OF THE PASTE II

DO YOUR TEETH GET DIRTY
WHEN YOU CLIMB UP AND
DOWN CHIMNEYS ALL NIGHT?
USE DENTOFRESH AND —

DON'T! USE TOOTHOFRESH.
IT'S MUCH BETTER.

NO, IT ISN'T !

YES, IT IS!

PUSH OFF, BOTH OF YOU.

WHO ARE YOU?

NEW, CLINICALLY
TESTED MINTOFRESH!

OH, NO! IN A NEW,
IMPROVED TUBE! AAAAH!

CHAPTER THIRTY

Santa's head came out of the chimney, and the rest of Santa followed.

He looked at them and smiled.

"Home," he said.

"Good on yourself, Santa," said Robbie.

"Over the North Pole, Rover," said Santa. "It's the quickest way."

"Now you're talking," said Rover.

Back into the air they went, and Rover turned and headed north and east.

Home.

They were tired and happy. They huddled together and stayed warm.

Home.

They flew over mountains and valleys made of ice, the most beautiful landscape on earth, but they were too tired to look.

Home.

CHAPTER THIRTY-ONE

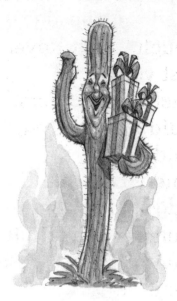

And here they were.

Flying out of the clouds over Dublin. The cacti that line the streets of the city saw them and waved.

"Well done," said a cactus.

"Medium rare!" said his girlfriend beside him.

They landed just as their parents were waking up.

Santa hugged them and climbed back into the sleigh.

"What's the story?" said Rover.

"Lapland, please, Rover," said Santa.

"Fair enough," said Rover. "But it's going to cost you."

"How much?" said Santa.

"Three quid," said Rover.

"One," said Santa.

"Two," said Rover.

"One fifty," said Santa

"One seventy-five," said Rover.

"One seventy-one," said Santa.

"One seventy-four."

"One seventy-two."

"One seventy-three."

"Done," said Santa. "Ho ho ho."

"Plus ten per cent service charge," said Rover. "Ho ho ho."

And he ran, and lifted himself on to the air. And, before the parents came out to the garden, the sleigh and Rover and Santa – "Ho ho ho!" – were gone.

"Bye-dee-bye, kids," said Hans.

"Come along, Hans," said Heidi.

And they wriggled in under their

bush just before Mister Mack arrived.

"Up already?" said Mister Mack.

What Mister Mack didn't know was, it was four o'clock in the afternoon. The day was nearly over.

"What did Santa bring you?" said Billie Jean.

"Eh."

Jimmy looked at Robbie.

"Eh."

Robbie looked at Jimmy.

"Who are you?" said Kayla.

"You didn't open them yet?" said Billie Jean.

"Bum-bum," said Victoria.

"You wanted to say Happy Christmas to each other first?" said Billie Jean. "Isn't that sweet?"

"Ah, there you are, Vicki-baa."

It was Tina.

"Hey, lads," said the bush. "Tina's in our garden."

"Oh, wow," said the shed. "Is my roof OK?"

She was with Celestine, Victoria's father. Celestine looked up at the sky.

"Notice anything?" he said.

They all looked.

"It isn't raining," he said.

And he was right. For the first time in four months it wasn't raining.

"And look!"

In Lagos, the Papa and the Mama sat in bed and shook their snow-domes.

And in Dublin, it had started to snow.

"Brilliant!" said Jimmy. "We can make a snowman."

Robbie put his hand out and caught a snowflake. Then he licked it off his hand.

"It isn't snow," he said. "It's sugar."

"Brilliant!" said Jimmy. "We can make a sugarman."

They all ran around the garden, the kids in their padded-up clothes and the adults in grown-up jammies and T-shirts. They chased and laughed and caught the falling sugar in their open hands and mouths.

The sugar was general all over Ireland. It was falling on every part of the dark central plain, on the treeless hills, falling softly upon the Bog of Allen. It was falling, too, on the baldy heads of little Irish men and women and on the mad cows that use new, improved Mintofresh.

Back in the garden, the kids were building a sugarman.

And what about their magic night with Santa? They'd forgotten all about it. When Santa had hugged them, he'd taken back their memories of the night. They remembered, but only in their dreams. Sometimes Jimmy would dream about flying through the clouds, and Kayla would bungee-jump into warm kitchens, and Robbie would fly over lion packs, and Victoria would kiss the foreheads of the Mama and the Papa in Lagos.

And, maybe because of that magic night, as they grew older and became teenagers, then grown-ups, they still did childish things, even when they became very old. Jimmy often farted under the bedclothes and giggled, even when he was eighty-three. Kayla rubbed her nose on other people's shoulders and left a trail of snot on them, even when she was thirty-eight. Robbie often rang on doorbells and ran away, even when he was ninety-one. And Victoria? She was still jumping out of upstairs windows when she was a hundred and twenty-seven.

ANOTHER ENDING

If you thought that ending was a bit soppy, here's a different one.

And maybe because of that magic night, as they grew older and became teenagers, then grown-ups, they got madder and madder and more and more crazy. Jimmy became the most famous bank robber in the world. He didn't just rob the money. He took the buildings as well. Kayla became a scientist and invented a way of bringing dead volcanoes back to life.

And she invented a microwave that could turn nuggets back into chickens. All over the world, mothers and fathers had heart attacks when they opened their microwave doors. Robbie became the president of Ireland and went all over the world meeting very important people. But that's not all he did. When he was having dinner with the very important people he'd climb in under the table and tie their laces together. Sixteen presidents and twenty-seven prime ministers broke their legs while Robbie was the president, and no one ever caught him. And Victoria? She was still throwing people out of upstairs windows, even when she was two hundred and twelve.

ANOTHER ONE

If the last ending was a bit too violent and crazy for you, and if you're a parent and you're worried about letting your child read the book, here's a different one.

And, maybe because of that magic night, as they grew older and became teenagers, then grown-ups, they all became fine, respectable citizens. Jimmy always lifted the toilet seat before going for a wee and never, ever did it on the floor – because it's very unhygienic and unfair to people who don't like sitting on wet toilet seats. Kayla always put her sweet papers in the bin and never, ever threw them on the ground – because it's a bad thing to do and it makes a mess and ruins the environment and it stops tourists from coming to Ireland to spend their money. Robbie always brushed his teeth and never, ever just wet the toothbrush and pretended that he'd brushed them – because that's a sneaky thing to do and it upsets the grown-ups and you'll need your teeth all your life, for eating food and biting sellotape. Robbie's motto was, "My teeth are my best friends." (By the way, he used new, clinically tested Mouthofresh, in the new, improved digital tube.) And Victoria? She was still closing upstairs windows in case someone fell out, even when she was three hundred and seventy-six.

THE REAL ENDING

After they'd made the sugarman, they went inside and had their dinner. And it was very nice, especially the spuds and gravy.

THE MESSAGEY BITS

All good stories have messages, and this one has eight of them. Here they are:

1. If your name is Dermot and you live in Sligo, your mammy says you're to hurry home because your dinner is getting cold.

2. If you're alone in the kitchen but you think there's someone looking at you, it might just be the fridge.

3. If you're standing at an upstairs window and a girl called Victoria runs into the room, be careful.

4. For healthy gums and that tingling fresh-breath feeling, use new improved Smilofresh, with new harmless fluoride.

5. If your name is Dermot and you live in Sligo, your mammy is getting very annoyed.

6. If you hear strange noises coming from your roof, it's probably Rover, practising for next Christmas.

7. If you're a fly and you live in a country that has no lizards, you should still have your passport ready – just in case.

8. If your name is Dermot and you live in Sligo, your mammy says she's given your dinner to the cat and it serves you right and you'll just have to make do with a bowl of cornflakes.
So there.

THE END

Hey, pal.

Oh, yes. Sorry Rover. I nearly forgot.

9. If you're a fine-looking collie and you live in Honolulu, Rover says *Aloha.*

THE END

Hey, Dermot. Your mammy isn't angry any more and when she said that she'd given your dinner to the cat she was telling a fib. It's lovely – chicken and spuds – and there's ice cream after. And, by the way, she has chocolates and other great stuff hidden in her handbag.

BIBLIOGRAPHY
If you liked this book, here are some more you might enjoy.

Rover Saves Easter
(Hound Dog Press)

Rover Saves Friday Afternoon 2
(Hound Dog Press)

Tuesdays with Rover
(Dog Poo Philosophy Press)

The Dog with the Golden Gun
(Armed Hound Books)

*Leave All Your Money to Your Dog: A Self-Help
Guide for Rich People Who Are Dying*
(Dog Poo Philosophy Press)

*Yo! I Bit Eminem's Leg!: The Confessions
of a Dogsta Rapper*
(Snoop Dog Books)

A Is for Ankle, B Is for Bite It: A Canine Dictionary
(Dogford University Press)

Rover Saves Easter Again
(Hound Dog Press)

How to Sniff Friends and Influence People
(Dog Poo Philosophy Press)

Rover Copperfield
(Kennel Classics)

All of these exciting titles are
available from *www.dogpoo.ie*
"Putting the woof back into reading."

This book was printed on paper. You probably think that paper is made from wood pulp. But it is not. Paper is, in fact, made from the teeth of little chipmunks. You might have enjoyed this book – we're glad – but twenty-seven chipmunks lost their teeth so that you could enjoy it. Reading a good book is a wonderful, once-in-a-lifetime experience, but have you ever tried chewing an acorn with your gums? Probably not. If you feel guilty about this, or even if you don't care, send all your money and all your parents' money and your brothers' and sisters' money to Save the Gummy Chipmunks, 74 Rover Villas, Killester, Dublin 5, Ireland.

This book was designed and art directed by Darren Kelly. "So what?" you ask. Well, Darren Kelly is a monkey, the very first Irish monkey to design a book. We're very proud of Darren. Brian Ajhar's artwork for the interior was created by accident and a pencil. The text was set in 15-point Kelly Roman, a typeface designed by Seamus Kelly, Darren Kelly's mother's brother – the monkey's uncle, in other words. He designed it in 1951, and did absolutely nothing else that year. The book was printed on a huge noisy machine that would probably kill you if it fell on you and was bound by Fluffy, Puffy and Cuddly, at the Home for Gummy Chipmunks, in Killester, Dublin.